Cinderella

Anne Cassidy and Jan McCafferty

W
FRANKLIN WATTS
LONDON•SYDNEY

Cumbria
County Council

Libraries, books and more . . .

Please return/renew this item by the last due date.
Library items may be renewed by phone on
030 33 33 1234 (24 hours) or via our website

www.cumbria.gov.uk/libraries

Cumbria Libraries
CLIC
Interactive Catalogue

Ask for a CLIC password

Chapter 1:
Sad Cinderella

Once upon a time, there was a girl called Cinderella. She was not happy and every day she cried.

Cinderella had two stepsisters. One was tall and was called Marigold. The other was small and was called Primrose. Primrose and Marigold hated Cinderella. They made her work all day long.

Marigold made
Cinderella
wear rags.

Primrose made her sleep by the fire
in the kitchen.

One day a letter arrived. "It's from the
prince," said Marigold. "What can it be?"
She was so excited as she opened the letter.
"Let me see," said Primrose, "Oh, look!
It's an invitation
to a ball at
the palace."

Cinderella smiled. "How wonderful,"
she thought, "a ball at the palace."
Everyone would have a good time.
There would be dancing! More than
anything, Cinderella loved to dance.

"But you can't come, Cinderella!"
Marigold said.

"Course you can't come," Primrose said,
"Everyone would laugh at you!"

"Look at silly Cinderella," Marigold sneered.

"In those horrible rags," Primrose sniggered.

They laughed

and laughed.

7

Chapter 2:
Fairy Godmother
to the Rescue

After her stepsisters had left for the ball, Cinderella sat by the fireplace.

She looked at her rags and her bare feet.
How silly she'd been to think she would
go to the ball.
"It's not fair," she sniffed, "I'd love to
go to the ball." She was miserable and
blinked hard to stop her tears.

Suddenly there was a big flash. Cinderella
jumped. It was a fairy with a wand!
Cinderella couldn't believe what she
was seeing.

"I'm your fairy godmother," the fairy said.
"You shall go to the ball, Cinderella."

The fairy godmother waved her wand.
The room filled with light and glitter.
In a flash, there was a new dress and
sparkling glass slippers.

Then the fairy godmother looked around the kitchen. She saw a pumpkin. "Just what I was looking for!" she said.

Then she saw four black mice. "Just what I need!" she said.

Then she saw a rat. "Perfect!" she cried.

The fairy godmother waved her wand
and, in a flash, there were four black horses,
a coach and a handsome coach driver.
"Here is your coach," she said, "It will take
you to the palace."

"Now I really can go to the ball,"
said Cinderella.

"Be back before the clock strikes twelve!"
said the fairy godmother.

"Bye bye!" Cinderella said.

She was happier than she had ever been.

"Don't forget to be back by twelve!"

the fairy godmother shouted.

Chapter 3:
The Prince's Ball

When Cinderella arrived at the ball, everyone looked at her. The lords and ladies were surprised.

"Who is she?" they wondered.

"Where did she come from?" they said.

"What's her name?" they cried.

The stepsisters were jealous.

"Look at that beautiful dress," Marigold moaned.

"Look at the way she stands," Primrose muttered. "She must be a princess from another land."

The stepsisters stared and stared.

The prince couldn't believe his eyes.

He looked at Cinderella for a long time.

"Will you dance with me?" he asked.

"Of course I will," Cinderella agreed,

"I love to dance. It is my favourite thing!"

The prince was thrilled. He took Cinderella's
hand and led her to the
centre of the
ballroom.

The prince and Cinderella danced.

The music stopped.

The prince said, "Oh please! Dance with me again!"

So the prince and Cinderella danced and danced and danced all night.

Suddenly Cinderella heard the clock strike twelve. She remembered what the fairy godmother had said.

"Oh no," she cried, "I have to go."

She ran out of the ballroom and straight out of the palace.

The prince chased after her but Cinderella was gone. He didn't know what to do.

Then, on the ground, he saw a glass slipper.
"Look! She left this behind!" he cried.
The prince thought and thought.
"Whoever can fit into the slipper
will be my princess,"
he promised.

Chapter 4:
The Prince's Quest

The prince walked up and down every street in the land. He searched every house.

"I will not give up," he said, "I will find the owner of the glass slipper."

One day he arrived at Cinderella's house.

His footman knocked politely on the door.

"I want to find the owner of this slipper!" the prince declared.

The slipper sat on a velvet cushion.
"I'll try it on!" Marigold said, grabbing it.
She tried it on. She pushed her foot in as
hard as she could.

But the slipper
was much too
small. Her foot
didn't fit into it.

"Ha! Ha!" said Primrose, "Let me have it!
It will fit me."

Primrose put
her foot into the
glass slipper but
it was much
too big.
The stepsisters
were furious.

"It doesn't fit either of you,"
the prince said, sadly. "I will
never find the owner of this shoe."
Then he saw a girl in rags sitting
by the fireplace.
"Let this girl try it on!" he said.
"But that's just Cinderella!" said Marigold.
"She doesn't even wear a proper dress!"
sniggered Primrose.

Cinderella sat down. She tried the glass
slipper on. It fitted perfectly.
The prince was delighted. He had found the
girl from the ball at last.

Chapter 5:
A Royal Wedding

The prince was in love with Cinderella.
"Will you be my princess?" he asked.
"I will. As long as we can dance a lot,"
Cinderella replied.
"As much as you like!" promised the prince.
The day of the wedding came. Cinderella
wore a beautiful dress. The prince looked
very smart. The people cheered. There was
music and a lot of dancing.

The stepsisters quarrelled and ate far too
much cake. The fairy godmother watched
it all. This time, she didn't need to use any
spells. The prince and Cinderella lived
happily ever after.

About the story

Cinderella is a European fairy tale. The most popular version of the story was published by Charles Perrault in 1697, and includes the pumpkin, the fairy godmother and the glass slipper. The Brothers Grimm also included a version of the tale in their collection of stories in 1812. The story of an unfortunate girl whose life is changed for the better is a common theme. The earliest version of *Cinderella* is considered to be a story called *Rhodopis* from the 1st century BCE. This story is about a Greek slave girl who marries the king of Egypt.

Be in the story!

Imagine you are Cinderella's stepsisters at her wedding to the prince. What might you be thinking?

Now imagine you are the prince and you must write a letter to the fairy godmother. What would you like to say to her?

First published in 2014 by
Franklin Watts
338 Euston Road
London
NW1 3BH

Franklin Watts Australia
Level 17/207 Kent Street
Sydney
NSW 2000

A CIP catalogue record for this book is available
from the British Library.

The artwork for this story first appeared in
Hopscotch Fairy Tales: Cinderella

ISBN 978 1 4451 2993 8 (hbk)
ISBN 978 1 4451 2994 5 (pbk)
ISBN 978 1 4451 2996 9 (library ebook)
ISBN 978 1 4451 2995 2 (ebook)

Series Editor: Jackie Hamley
Series Advisor: Catherine Glavina
Series Designer: Cathryn Gilbert

Printed in China

Franklin Watts is a divison of
Hachette Children's Books,
an Hachette UK company.
www.hachette.co.uk